The Adv... Veggie & Angus Burger

By: Robert Magliano

The Adventures of Veggie & Angus Burger
Copyright © 2017 Robert Magliano. All rights reserved.

Published by Mindstir Media LLC
45 Lafayette Rd. Suite 181 | North Hampton, NH 03862 | USA
1.800.767.0531 | www.mindstirmedia.com

Printed in the United States of America
ISBN-13: 978-0-9991507-1-9
Library of Congress Control Number: 2017953179

Dedication:

To my grandmother.

In a small kitchen in Foodsville, twin sliders were born. Their names were Veggie and Angus.

The twins were happy as could be.
They were the best of friends, constantly
laughing and playing with one another.

Veggie and Angus were inseparable.
They were in the same classroom at
school and even shared the same friends.

Every day after school, Veggie and Angus walked home together, talking about their favorite part of the day.

Angus said that his
favorite part of the day
was playing sports at recess.

Veggie told Angus that she
liked science and math class.

Even though the twins were
good at different things, they were
always there to help each other out.

As the twins grew from sliders to burgers, they continued to walk home from school together and talk about the favorite part of their days.

After summer break, Veggie and Angus were both excited and nervous for their first day back to school because they were going to be in different classrooms for the very first time.

Even though they were in different classrooms, they still planned to walk home together and tell each other about their favorite part of the day.

Veggie's first class of the day was English.
Veggie was great at spelling and was
asked to be on the spelling team.

In gym class, Angus discovered
that he was a great athlete.

When it was time for lunch, the guys
from the school baseball team called
Angus to sit with them.

Before Veggie could sit down, her new friends Arnie Artichoke and Sarah Squash pointed to a spot for her to sit with the other kids on the spelling team.

After school, Angus waited by Veggie's classroom so they could walk home together. Benjamin Bacon and Dan Dumpling yelled for Angus to join them for baseball practice, but he waited for his sister.

As they walked home, Angus and Veggie told each other about their new friends.

Veggie asked Angus to sit with her new friends during lunch, but Angus wanted Veggie to sit with his new friends. Veggie didn't want to sit with a pound of meatheads. Angus did not want to sit with a basket of plants.

Each week, Veggie and Angus enjoyed hanging out with their new friends.

In fact, they often acted like they didn't know each other at school.

After a few weeks of school it was time for Angus' first big baseball game. The score was tied. The team had one last chance to win. Angus was up to bat.

The pitcher threw the ball and

Whack

The ball went over the fence.
Homerun!

Angus was carried off the field by the team and was the hero of the game.

Even though his team had won the game, Angus didn't feel happy. He wanted to share the moment with his sister.

The next day, Veggie had her first spelling competition. She was so nervous that she thought she was going to be sick. She walked to the podium and waited for the announcer to give her the word to spell.

She spelled the first word and got it right!
Then she spelled the second, and the third and
the fourth words right. She took a deep breath,
then spelled the final word and got it right!

The team was awarded first place and Veggie was named the team's MVP. She looked out in the crowd and noticed that Angus was not there to celebrate her big day.

Veggie was sad because Angus had
always been there to cheer her on.

Veggie walked home alone
and thought about how
much she missed her brother.

After school the next day, Angus left baseball
practice and noticed Veggie was walking
home alone. Angus went to ketchup with
her so they could walk home together.

Angus told Veggie about the baseball game
and how he had hit the game winning homerun.
Veggie told Angus about the spelling competition
and how she helped the team win.

The twins were sad. If only they had been there to see each other help their teams win. At the same time, they stopped and mustard up the courage to tell each other they were sorry.

Veggie and Angus agreed that no matter what, family comes first and that they would always be there for one another. They knew that they could accomplish anything with family by their side.

The End

CPSIA information can be obtained
at www.ICGtesting.com
Printed in the USA
BVHW022049081221
623541BV00002B/48